KT-468-735

STATUS: FILE CLOSED
LOCATION:
HIMACHAL PRADESH, INDIA
CODE NAME: PANI

STATUS: FILE CLOSED
LOCATION:
SICHUAN, CHINA
CODE NAME: JING JING

STATUS: FILE CLOSED
LOCATION:
SOUTH BORNEO
CODE NAME: KAWAN

STATUS: FILE CLOSED
LOCATION:
SUMATRA, INDONESIA
CODE NAME: TORA

STATUS: FILE CLOSED
LOCATION:
KENYA, AFRICA
CODE NAME: TOMBOI

RESCUE
MISSION DATABASE

CHAPTER ONE

"Yahoo!" yelled Zoe, as she swung her go-kart round the tight, floodlit bend and powered off along the straight. There was no way Ben was going to catch her now. She'd win this race for sure. There was only one more lap to go.

But to her surprise, someone was flagging her down.

The track must be closing early, thought Zoe. She braked hard and pulled in.

She was just taking off her crash helmet when Ben came screeching to a halt

7

behind her. They ran over to the blonde-haired woman holding the flag. Zoe recognized her immediately.

"Erika!" she cried in excitement. She looked round to make sure that no one else was in earshot. "Have we got a new mission?"

Ben and Zoe Woodward were the youngest operatives in Wild, a top secret organization run by their godfather, Dr Stephen Fisher. Erika Bohn was his second-in-command. Whenever there was news of an animal in danger, the eleven-year-old twins would drop everything and fly off to its rescue. Their missions took them to some amazing – and dangerous – places.

"Yes," said Erika. "I'm here to take you straight to your destination." She grinned. "Sorry I interrupted your race."

"No problem," said Ben, cheerfully. "We'll call that last one a draw, Zoe."

"We will not!" exclaimed his sister.

"I was in the lead all the way!"

But Ben had jumped into his kart and zoomed off to return it.

Five minutes later they were speeding along in Erika's car towards a private airfield. Ben quickly sent a text message to their grandmother, who was looking after them while their parents were working abroad as vets. Gran was in on the secret of Wild and very proud of her daring grandchildren. A reply flashed up on Ben's phone.

Have fun and be careful. Gran xx

"It's great we're off on a new mission," said Zoe, watching from the front seat as they passed bare fields and winter trees, lit briefly in the car's headlights. "It'll make our Christmas holidays much more exciting – although I hate to think of animals being in trouble. I wonder which one we're going to be helping this time."

"You know the drill," said Erika. "Look in the glove compartment and you'll find a clue from your godfather."

Zoe pulled out a glass eyeball and inspected it in the beam of a torch she found there. The eyeball had an orangey-brown iris with a round, black pupil.

"It reflects the light," she said, as she twisted it about. "So it's possibly an animal that needs to see well at night."

Ben reached over from the back and took it from her, along with the torch.

"And it's a good size so it's probably one of the big cats."

"I agree," said Zoe. "Let's see what Uncle Stephen has to say."

Ben gave her the eyeball and Zoe placed it into a hole in the dashboard. The small hologram of a man immediately appeared in the air in front of them. He wore a white lab coat and had a straw hat plonked on top of a mop of red hair.

"Greetings, Godchildren!" said the figure. "Destination Africa for this mission…"

"Definitely not a tiger on that continent," said Ben.

"…and Africa is a *king*-sized clue to the animal you'll be rescuing," Uncle Stephen went on. "Get in touch as soon as you know the answer."

The hologram disappeared.

"A king-sized clue," repeated Zoe. "Then it's got to be—"

"The *king* of the beasts!" interrupted Ben. "Wow! We're rescuing a lion. That'll be amazing – and a bit scary."

"Your BUGs are in the door pocket," Erika told them. "You can contact Dr Fisher with your answer."

Ben and Zoe never went on a mission without their BUGs: the Brilliant Undercover Gizmos invented by their godfather. They looked like hand-held computer consoles, but had lots of wonderful applications from satellite maps and communicators to animal tracking devices. Zoe took hers, hit the hot key for Wild HQ and turned on speakerphone.

"Good evening, Ben and Zoe!" came their godfather's voice. "Worked it out yet?"

"We have," said Zoe. "It's a lion."

"Well done," boomed Dr Fisher. "You're off to the Kalahari Desert in Namibia."

"Awesome!" said Ben.

"James here at HQ has picked up a news report on Namibian radio," their godfather went on. "A lioness has been seen prowling round a well for a few days. She's very agitated. It's causing a problem as this is the only clean water around for the local people and they daren't go near."

"Lionesses aren't usually found on their own, are they?" said Zoe, puzzled.

"I don't think this one is alone," explained Uncle Stephen. "There are also reports of strange sounds coming from the well. The news reporter said the tribespeople think it's haunted."

"Have you started ghost hunting, Uncle Stephen?" said Ben, grinning.

There was the sound of a chuckle. "No, no!" came Dr Fisher's voice. "There's a much simpler explanation."

"It's most likely that one of the lioness's cubs has fallen down the well and is calling to her," said Erika, swinging the car through some gates on to a rough track. "That would explain the ghostly sounds and also why she won't leave."

"Oh, the poor cub!" sighed Zoe.

"So we're going to rescue it!" said Ben.

"And return it to its mother as soon as possible," said Uncle Stephen. "The cub will starve to death otherwise. We don't know how long it's been down the well, or whether it's injured. That's why you're flying straight there."

"We need to preserve as many Namibian lions as we can, especially the young ones," Erika told them. "The numbers have been declining because of disease – and humans, unfortunately. People are illegally hunting lions and there are cases of them being poisoned when they stray too near to farms."

"You should get to Namibia by breakfast, local time," Uncle Stephen went on. "Your equipment's already on board the Wild Jet. There'll be plenty of time on the journey for you to sleep and watch a desert training video."

"We learned about sandstorms in the climate chamber last time we were at Wild HQ," Ben reminded him.

"And that could be very important," replied their godfather. "But you need to be able to survive ordinary desert conditions, too. The Kalahari is a hostile place at the best of times. I'm glad you won't be out there long. Good luck. Over and out."

Erika brought the car to a halt next to a small plane that stood on an airstrip.

"You'll be taking a vetkit in case the cub needs attention," she said, as they jumped out, "and tranquillizer guns, of course."

"Too right." Ben nodded. "We don't want the lioness eating us while we're trying to rescue her cub!"

"How about ropes to climb down the well?" asked Zoe.

Erika nodded and swung open the door of the plane to let the children clamber aboard. "And there's lightweight clothing that reflects the sun to help keep you cool. It's summer out there – and very hot."

"What's our new gadget, Erika?" asked Ben eagerly. "Uncle Stephen always comes up with something amazing for our missions."

"Your godfather's really excited about his latest invention," said Erika, strapping herself into her seat belt and making her final take-off checks. "But you can't see it until we get to Namibia."

"Then what are we waiting for?" declared Zoe.

CHAPTER TWO

"Wow!" exclaimed Zoe, as she and Ben jumped down from the Wild Jet, and gazed all about them. Small bushes and plants pushed up through the red sandy soil of the Kalahari Desert, and in the distance, smooth dunes rose like hills. The morning sun was just peeping above them, casting long shadows over the land.

Ben tried on the goggles he'd found in his backpack. The tinted glasses curved round to fit closely to his face.

"These are cool," he said, striking a pose

as if he was in a catalogue. "They're what sportsmen wear."

"They're sun and sand goggles," said Erika, as she climbed down from the cockpit. "In case of sandstorms. Your godfather has fitted them with a zoom function so you won't need binoculars – and you'll find a built-in spotlight in the middle to help you see the cub down the well. How's the desert clothing?"

"A perfect fit," said Zoe, doing a twirl in her lightweight shirt and trousers, "and very comfortable."

"Can we see our new gadget now?" asked Ben impatiently.

"Of course," said Erika, walking to the rear of the plane. "I'd like to have landed closer to the well," she told them, "but this is the nearest strip of land that's free of rocks. You'll have a few kilometres to travel so you'll be needing … a WASP."

"A wasp?" snorted Ben. "That's the last thing we need."

Erika smiled at him and pulled a lever. A hatch slowly opened and a ramp slid down until it was resting on the sand. She climbed up into the dark hold. The next minute she appeared again, dragging something covered in a tarpaulin down the ramp.

"This is the WASP," declared Erika, pulling back the cover with a flourish. "The Wind and Solar-powered Pod."

The children gazed in excitement at the sleek, boat-shaped vehicle in front of them. It had a light frame with two seats, a small motor at the back, a gear stick and a steering wheel like a go-kart's.

"A sand buggy!" exclaimed Ben. "I've always wanted to try one of those."

"This is no ordinary sand buggy," said Erika. She reached into the framework, erected a telescopic mast and ran a shiny silver sail up it. "This works the same way as a sail on a boat," she told them. "The sail also acts as a solar panel. Even when it's folded to the mast it absorbs enough light to charge the engine battery. So, when there's no wind, you won't get stuck without power."

"It's awesome," cried Ben, going over to inspect the controls. "How fast does it go? After all, we might need to outrun a lion. They can get up to speeds of eighty kilometres an hour over short distances, you know."

Zoe rolled her eyes and Erika laughed. "It can't do that. Dr Fisher told me to warn you to take it steady, Ben. He's designed it to get you to your destination – not to race lions."

Ben grinned. "I'll be careful. And I'm glad it's not a camel." He pulled a face as he remembered his last painful ride in Africa. "I should be able to stay on board this."

Erika unloaded their backpacks.

"Hope there's lots of food," said Ben.

"You and your stomach!" exclaimed Zoe.

"There's the usual rations," Erika assured them, "and special powdered formula for the cub in case the mum isn't there to take over right away."

"Did you know lions aren't weaned until they're about six months old," piped up Ben. "Though they do start eating meat before that."

Zoe sighed. "Thank you, Mr Handy Factman."

"You'll just need to add water to the bottle for the cub's milk," said Erika. "There's a water tank under the WASP frame. Remember to drink plenty yourselves. It's easy to get dehydrated out here."

Ben stowed their packs in the storage compartment behind the seats. "I can't wait to get going."

"Good!" said Erika. "I'm off to a wildlife park in Botswana now. There's been an outbreak of blue tongue disease in the deer and antelope, and your godfather has developed a faster-acting vaccine. I'm delivering the first batch."

"I've heard Mum and Dad talking about blue tongue disease," said Zoe. "It can be fatal."

Ben nodded. "And if the deer and the antelope die out that means there's less prey for predators like lions."

"Talking of predators, we mustn't forget our scent dispersers, Ben," said Zoe, scrolling through her BUG menu. "We don't want to attract anything that fancies meals-on-wheels."

Ben activated his scent disperser and jumped into the WASP's driving seat.

"Hang on a minute," said Zoe indignantly. "I was the champion go-karter. I should drive."

"You can do the sailing," replied Ben, with a grin. "I'll admit you're better than me at *that*."

"Keep your tranquillizer guns at the ready at all times," warned Erika.

Zoe nodded and climbed in beside her brother. "Don't worry, we will."

She took the guns from the backpacks and put them in the dip behind their seats. Then she called up the satellite map on her BUG. "It looks as if we have to go east to get to the well." She pointed to a clump of trees with gnarled trunks, beyond which rose the distant sand dunes. "Just about there, I reckon."

"We'll need the engine," said Ben. "There's not much wind here."

Zoe put down the sail, then Ben flicked a switch and the motor whirred gently into life.

"Bye, Erika!" called Zoe. "We'll contact you the minute we've got the cub back to its mother. Shouldn't be too long." She turned to her brother. "Nice and slow, Ben."

Ben grinned. "As if I'd do anything else!"

CHAPTER THREE

As soon as Erika climbed into the plane, Ben put his foot on the accelerator. The WASP skidded across the bumpy earth, swerved from side to side and stopped with a jolt. Ben looked at his sister's shocked face and burst out laughing.

"Only kidding! I'll take it steady from now on."

He set off again, this time steering the vehicle slowly and expertly between the small boulders that littered the hard, red earth. Already the temperature was rising.

The children both pulled on their peaked caps with flaps that covered their necks.

"Look!" Zoe clutched at Ben's arm. "There's something moving over there." She put her glasses on zoom. "Hyenas. There's no mistaking the way they hunch their backs. Let's not get too close."

Ben steered the WASP round a group of rough brown trees growing straight up and topped with small yellow leaves.

"Check those out!" he said. "I read about them on the plane. Elephant's trunk plants

– and they look just like them!"

"This is a very strange place," said Zoe, as they wove among low plants and sparse patches of grass. "There's more vegetation than I expected."

The sun rose in the sky and a light breeze blew up.

"Time to put the wind to use," said Ben.

"Then you'd better let the expert take control," said Zoe.

Ben gave her a mock salute. "Aye, aye, Captain! You can do the sailing any time."

He brought the WASP to a stop and flicked a switch to turn off the engine. Zoe clambered into the driver's seat and released the sail. It billowed out and caught the wind, and soon the WASP was tacking from side to side across the bumpy ground.

"Awesome!" yelled Zoe. "Almost as good as sailing."

"Better!" Ben yelled back.

He checked the map, holding tightly to his BUG as they jolted along. "We're nearly there," he said. "Just another kilometre or so."

"There's a hollow up ahead," said Zoe, peering out over the shimmering landscape. "And I can hear goats."

"Better check it out," said Ben. "There could be people looking after their herd down there. We might need to change our route so they don't see us."

"I agree," said Zoe. "Two children

travelling on their own out here? They'd
be bound to tell us it's not safe and try to
stop us. They wouldn't know we're on a
vital mission."

"And we couldn't tell them," said Ben.

Zoe let the sail flap loose and braked so
that the buggy came to rest behind a clump
of thorny bushes.

They crept across the hot sand to where
the land dipped away. Using the bushes
and grass as cover, they gazed down at a
herd of goats. They were grazing at the
bottom of the hollow, watched over by
two small figures.

"They're only children," said Ben. "Let's
speak to them."

"Do you think we should?" Zoe answered
doubtfully. "We don't want to attract
attention to ourselves."

"But it could be useful," insisted Ben.
"If we can make ourselves understood they

could give us some information. They must
know the well. They might be able to tell
us if the lioness is still there."

"Translators in so we can understand
everything we hear," said Zoe, peeling off
the small rubber earpiece from the side of
her BUG and popping it into her ear. She
scrolled through the menu. "I looked it up
on the plane. They speak a form of click
language called Nama, although many
Namibians speak English as well." She found
Nama and entered it. "Right, let's go."

They slipped their BUGs into their
pockets and set off towards the grazing
herd. The two children stood close by.
One was a girl of about Ben and Zoe's age.
Her hair was tightly woven into plaits
close to her head and she wore a bright red
T-shirt over a wrap-around skirt. The other
goatherd was a boy of about five. The girl
held a long spear.

"Hello!" called Ben, as he and Zoe approached.

The goatherds looked up and stared at them solemnly.

"Can you help us?" said Zoe, slowly. "We are visitors in your country."

The children glanced at each other but didn't speak.

"We have come a long way," added Ben. "We are thirsty."

He clutched his throat and stuck out his tongue. "Water!" he croaked.

The girl took a jar, bound in cowhide and without a word handed it to Ben.

"Thank you," he said, taking a small sip.

Then he handed it to Zoe who did the same. It had been a useful excuse to talk to the children, but they didn't want to leave them short of water in this hot, dry landscape. Ben rummaged in his backpack and pulled out two of Uncle Stephen's special energy bars. He passed them to the girl who inspected the wrappings.

"Cherry," she read slowly.

"You speak English?" said Zoe.

The girl nodded. "A little," she said. "But my brother not."

She handed a bar to the little boy, who unwrapped it quickly and began to eat.

He turned to his sister. "I like it," he said in his click language.

Ben and Zoe had to pretend they hadn't understood. Then he beamed at them, nodded his head and rubbed his tummy, and they grinned back.

"I'm Ben and this is my sister, Zoe," said Ben.

"My name is Tukwenethi," said the girl. She waved a hand towards her brother. "And that is Jossy."

"Thank you for the water," said Zoe, handing back the bottle. "Is it from a well or a pool?" she added, trying to think of a way to bring the talk round to the lioness.

"All our water is from wells," replied Tukwenethi. She pointed to the northern horizon. "There is pool there. But is bad water. Make people ill. Only animals drink that."

"Is your well far away?" asked Ben.

"Not far," Tukwenethi said. "Two hours' walk. But we cannot use it. There is lion mother there. Now we have to go to next well, one day's walk, as she will not let us get near."

Her brother pulled at her arm and she told him what had been said in their language. His eyes widened.

"There's a ghost in the well!" His words echoed in the earpieces. "It moans and cries out. Mummy said someone was brave and went last night and it was still there. *I* would be brave and fight a lioness, but not a ghost."

Ben and Zoe gave each other a secret glance. The cub was alive last night!

Jossy spun round and stared up at the far side of the hollow.

Now Ben and Zoe could hear something as well. Adult voices, speaking in Nama, and they were heading their way.

They looked at each other in alarm. They each knew what the other was thinking. They had to disappear – and quickly!

CHAPTER FOUR

Tukwenethi turned to see where the voices were coming from, shading her eyes from the glare of the sun.

"We've got to go," whispered Ben. "If we go back out of the hollow the way we came, we'll be hidden by the bushes."

"But the children will see us leave," Zoe whispered back.

"I'll make sure they forget about us for a moment." Ben scrolled through the menu on his BUG. "Sorry, goats, you're about to see a predator!"

He pointed his BUG towards the herd and at once the hologram of a cheetah appeared in the middle of them. The terrified creatures skittered about, bleating in alarm.

Spear raised, Tukwenethi and her brother ran to see what was wrong.

"Job done," whispered Ben, snapping off the image before the two goatherds could spot it. "Come on!"

Ben and Zoe scrambled up the side of the hollow and hid behind a bush. They watched as two men hurried down to see why the goats were so agitated. The moment the children couldn't see them any more, they darted back to the WASP.

"I feel bad about not saying goodbye to Tukwenethi and Jossy," said Zoe. "But we must get on with our mission. Jossy will probably think we were the ghosts from the well now we've vanished into thin air."

"Ghosts who gave him a cherry energy bar!" replied Ben.

Zoe pulled the sail until it caught the wind, released the brake and they were off again.

Ben checked the satellite map on his BUG. "The well's just a short ride by WASP."

"We'll have done the rescue before lunch!" said Zoe cheerfully.

"*Now* who's thinking of food," Ben teased her, as they bumped across the desert.

The bushes were scarcer now and the ground became sandier as the WASP sped along towards the dunes. The red sand shimmered in the heat of the morning sun.

"The well should be in sight soon," yelled Zoe, adjusting the WASP's course to catch the breeze.

Ben checked his tranquillizer gun. "As soon as we're in range of the mother, slow down and I'll send her to sleep. We'll give her the smallest dose we can. We want her to wake quickly so that she can look after her cub once we've rescued it."

"There's the well," called Zoe. "It's up ahead."

A rough dirt track led across the dusty, open ground to a small stone mound with a simple wooden framework above. A pulley was fixed to it and a rope trailed down into the well.

"I can't see the lioness, though," said Ben, looking all around. "Where is she?"

"Probably gone to hunt for some food," whispered Zoe. "We're going to have to be careful. She could be back any moment."

She let the WASP roll slowly along the track towards the well, checking for any signs of movement. She brought it to a halt and jumped out, folding up the sail and hurriedly snatching up a tranquillizer gun.

She watched as Ben took a rope from the back of the buggy and ran over to the well.

Every flutter of leaves in the scrubby bushes had Zoe whirling round and gripping the gun tightly. She felt her heartbeat thundering in her ears.

"I hope nothing's happened to the cub since last night," she whispered anxiously. "It could have fallen into the water and drowned."

Ben switched on the spotlight on his glasses and peered down into the narrow circle of darkness. "I can't make out anything yet," he said, shining the light this way and that. "It's really deep and full of rocky ledges. Wait a minute. Did you hear something?"

Zoe tensed, concentrating on listening. Yes, there it was – an unearthly wailing echoing up from the depths.

"The cub's still alive!" she said in relief.

"But I'm not surprised the local people think the well's haunted. It doesn't sound like an animal at all. You climb down the well and I'll stand on guard. But be quick."

Ben inspected the pulley hanging from the wooden framework. "That might be strong enough for a bucket, but not one of us."

"Then we tie the rope to the WASP," said Zoe. "We can wedge it against the well."

Ben brought the sand buggy over to the stone wall and fixed the rope to the frame of the vehicle.

"Freeze!" hissed Zoe suddenly, raising the tranquillizer gun. "The lioness is back."

Scarcely daring to breathe, the children watched as a large animal emerged from behind a rock. She had a long, sleek body and her powerful muscles rippled under her golden coat as she moved. Tail swishing, she padded purposefully towards the well.

"Can you dart her from there?" muttered Ben between clenched teeth.

Zoe shook her head. "She's head on. I'll try to get to the side."

The big cat stopped as she caught sight of the children and gave a low, deep-throated, rumbling growl. Zoe's finger tightened on the trigger and she edged away from the well, keeping the gun trained on the lioness.

But the creature suddenly crouched, ready to attack. Zoe had to shoot *now*!

As the dart struck her flank, the terrified animal snarled and whipped round to see what had attacked her. The next second she was bounding towards the children. Ben and Zoe backed away in fright. For one terrible moment it looked as if the dart had had no effect. But then her steps faltered. Dragging herself up on to the stones of the well, the lioness slumped down, her head lolling over the opening.

Gingerly Ben crept up to her. She was sleeping deeply now. He felt a thrill of fear at being so close to this deadly predator.

"She was trying to protect her baby,"

whispered Zoe. "If only she knew we're here to help." She gently touched the lioness's soft ear. "We'll soon have your little one out of there," she murmured.

"Let's get on with it," said Ben. "We don't have long."

Zoe sat on the WASP, gathered up the loose rope and held it tightly. "I'll play it out as you go down," she said.

"And then you can reverse the WASP and pull me back up," said Ben. "I'll give two tugs when I'm ready."

Ben took the free end of the rope and tied it around his legs and waist, making a harness. He eased his legs over the edge of the well and found a foothold. Giving Zoe a thumbs up to let more of the rope go slack, he began to squeeze past the warm, limp lioness. At that moment, the sleeping animal gave a gurgle in her throat and her muzzle twitched, revealing a row of huge, sharp teeth. Ben froze. Surely the tranquillizer wasn't wearing off already?

The lioness's mouth relaxed and she was still again. Ben took a deep breath to calm himself and edged his way into the well, searching for foot- and handholds in the rough stone. The air was cool and damp.

He stopped and peered down. Far below, the water gleamed in his spotlight. His stomach lurched – the well was much deeper than he'd realized. He moved his head, trying to locate the cub. He couldn't see anything, so he began to climb down.

The sides of the well were slippery. Ben knew that he would have to take it slowly or he'd fall. He inched his way down, wedging his fingers into tiny crevices. At last he paused to rest. Above him was a tiny circle of sky, broken by the outline of the lioness's head. He shone his light down and caught sight of a little ledge near the bottom. The

glint of two round eyes
reflected back at him.
He'd found the cub!

Suddenly the narrow sides
of the well seemed to be
pressing in on him, and
he began to feel hot and
panicky. He wasn't sure
he could go any further.

Then he heard a faint,
pitiful mew. Forgetting
his fears, Ben climbed on
down towards the sound.

The cub was lying on the
ledge. By Ben's spotlight,
he could see its soft, golden
fur, the dark spots on its head
and every rib sticking out of
its body. It raised its head
weakly as he dropped into
the narrow space next to it.

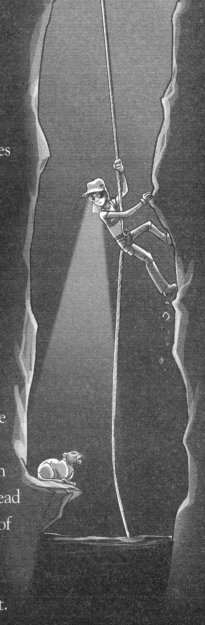

"We're going to get you back to your mum," he told the little creature, "and no more hide-and-seek down wells!"

Ben slowly reached out, took it by the scruff of its neck and held it tightly in one arm. The cub barely struggled.

He gave the signal on the rope and at once heard the distant whir of the WASP engine echoing down the stone walls as Zoe backed up the buggy. The rope tightened and he felt himself being hauled up towards the welcome light.

At last he could feel the warmth of the sun on his head and shoulders. He was about to reach for the edge of the well to haul himself up when he realized he was level with the face of the lioness. The bleary eyes were flickering open.

And now the huge creature was awake, and staring right at him.

CHAPTER FIVE

Ben could feel the cub struggling weakly in his arms as it smelt the familiar scent of its mother. Any second now she would realize her baby was there... *And then what?* came his terrified thought. If he moved, the lioness would attack.

Zoe watched in horror as the lioness stirred. She couldn't leave the buggy. Without her weight holding it in position, Ben and the cub would fall back down the well.

The rumbling in the animal's throat grew louder and more threatening. Then the lioness got to her feet and turned to face Zoe! There was only one thing to do. She had to tranquillize the mother again. Zoe raised the gun and fired. The lioness stumbled and fell lifelessly to the ground.

Ben hauled himself and the cub over the edge of the well. As soon as the rope went slack, Zoe jumped off the WASP, and ran over to help him out.

"Are you OK?" she asked. "You're shaking."

"I thought she was going for you," said Ben, laying the little cub gently on the ground.

"No way," replied his sister with a grin. "She didn't stand a chance against my super-quick trigger finger." She gazed at the baby lion. "You are beautiful!" she murmured, stroking the soft fur on its big, floppy paws. "Although you need a good meal. Let's check you out then beat a hasty retreat before your mum wakes again."

They knelt beside it.

"It doesn't look too bad, considering the poor thing fell quite a way," said Ben, checking the cub over. "The ledge was near the water so I reckon he's been able to get a drink at least. And you're a boy, aren't you?" He set the cub on his feet. The little creature tried to take a step and collapsed.

"Is he too weak to walk?" asked Zoe, gathering him up. "Wait, what's this?"

A deep gash ran down the inside of his left front leg.

The cub mewed and struggled weakly as Ben inspected the wound. "It's nasty," he said. "It needs treatment."

"Then we have to help him," said Zoe decisively. "There's no way we can leave him with his mum. They'll never get back to the pride. They'll be travelling so slowly they'll be sitting targets for any predators around. And this cut could get infected."

Ben nodded. "Looks like our mission has changed. We need to sort this leg out…"

"…and take him back to his family ourselves," finished Zoe. "If we can find the pride he comes from, that is." She glanced round at the dry, dusty desert, baking in the heat. "This was supposed to be the end of our mission. Now we don't know how long we'll be out in the Kalahari."

"We'll be OK," said Ben firmly. "We've got the kit, and plenty of food and water." He stroked the soft fur under the young lion's chin and then got to his feet. "We'll let Wild know of our change of plan, but first things first. Let's get out of range of our friend over there." He jerked a thumb towards the lioness. "I don't want to be around when she wakes up and smells her son. There's not enough wind to make a fast getaway – so I'll drive."

"Suits me," said Zoe. She picked up the cub and climbed on to the WASP, making him comfortable on her lap. "I'm going to call you Jossy, after the boy we met earlier." She stroked his soft fur. "I'm sorry we have to take you away from your mum for a little while, but it's for your own good."

Ben joined her and switched on the engine. "I say we head for the pool that

Tukwenethi told us about. She said all the animals go there. So it's a good bet that Jossy's pride drink at it too."

"I'll find it on the BUG," said Zoe. She held it up above the little cub and began to scroll through for the satellite map. "And it's likely that's where his mum will head when she wakes up and realizes her baby has gone. But hopefully not until we're far away."

"We'll have to make sure she doesn't catch us up then," said Ben.

"It took you ages to get down the well and back," said Zoe. "And she only woke up when you were nearly out. So she should be asleep about the same amount of time again." Then a thought hit her. "The lioness won't know we've taken her cub, Ben. She might stay at the well for ever. How can we get her back to the pride too?"

"Good point," said Ben. "We can't give

her a lift as well! We'll have to leave her
a trail." He reached over the side of the
WASP and picked up a handful of stones.
"If we rub these against Jossy's fur, we can
drop them every now and then. Hopefully
she'll pick up the scent and come after
her cub."

"And if we start the trail just near here
where Jossy's been standing, she'll set off in
the right direction," agreed Zoe.

"I'd better put my foot down," said Ben,
reversing the WASP away from the well,
"so she doesn't catch us up."

"You need to head north-west," said Zoe,
pointing. She flicked through her BUG
menu. "But I'm going to fire a tracking dart
into our lioness first. So we can keep an eye
on where she's got to."

"Good idea!"

Ben circled the WASP round the well as
Zoe aimed. As soon as the little dart had

been fired off, he turned the wheel and they were away. An orange light pulsed next to the well on Zoe's screen.

"Poor lioness," she murmured. "I've made her into a pincushion with all my shots."

They travelled on. Every now and then, Zoe rubbed a stone against Jossy's cheek and dropped it over the side.

She checked the tracking signal. "Mum's not woken up yet," she told Ben.

"Then I reckon it's safe to stop and see to Jossy's leg," said Ben, bringing the WASP to a halt by the thick trunk of a baobab tree. Its fan-like branches cast a small shade under the midday sun. "It'll be good to be sheltered from the heat for a while."

Ben mixed Uncle Stephen's special powdered formula with water and tried to feed it to the cub.

"He should be really hungry, but he's hardly taking any," cried Zoe in alarm.

"Maybe his leg's hurting him," suggested
Ben. He checked the wound. "I'm not a
vet," he said, "but it looks too deep to
leave."

"Let's ask Uncle Stephen what to do,"
said Zoe. "We need to tell him what's
happened anyway."

Ben took his BUG and hit the hot key for Wild HQ.

"Hello!" came their godfather's voice. "Have you reunited the little cub with his mum yet?"

Ben told him about their change of plan.

"Quick thinking, you two," said Dr Fisher. "But don't forget that leaving a scent trail can attract all sorts of predators. So you've got to have your wits about you at all times. I'll let Erika know you've been delayed. You can contact her when you're ready for a lift home."

"Before you go we need some advice," Zoe called into the speaker. "We think the gash needs stitches."

Ben held the BUG over the deep cut, took a photo and sent it to Uncle Stephen.

"Looks nasty," said their godfather. "But you can glue that together."

Ben and Zoe looked at each other, puzzled.

Then Zoe hit her forehead with her hand. "Of course!" she said. "Mum and Dad often use special medical glue for wounds. Mum showed me once on a horse that had cut its flank."

Ben searched in the vetkit and pulled out a small tube of ointment. "Woundbond," he read.

"That's it," said Uncle Stephen. "Give the cut a good wash, and stick it together with that. Then a dose of antibiotics – I know you can give those. Over and out… Oh, and watch you don't glue your fingers together – it's powerful stuff!"

Filling a syringe with water and antiseptic, Ben squirted the wound until he was sure that it was clean and applied the glue. Zoe carefully squeezed its edges together.

Jossy barely moved.

"That's amazing!" exclaimed Zoe, after a few minutes. "It's stuck already. It's like superglue." She scratched the little cub gently between the ears as Ben gave him an antibiotic injection. "You'll soon be on your feet, Jossy."

Ben looked out over the surrounding desert. "Better get going," he said. "We don't want Mum to catch us up."

Zoe nodded. "I'll keep checking her signal as we go."

Soon the WASP was bumping along over the rough ground. The sun was high in the sky now. The dunes stretched away to their right, brilliant red in the glaring light. Straight ahead the ground was flat, with a few scrubby bushes growing amongst the small rocks. Zoe rubbed another pebble on Jossy's fur and threw it behind them.

Ben wiped his forehead. "It's like being in

an oven," he complained, taking a swig
from his water bottle.

Zoe peered through her goggles, adjusting
them to zoom. "It's so hot there's hardly any
animals around," she reported. "Some
giraffes way over there. And a flock of birds
hovering above the trees down to the
south."

"I suppose most creatures are waiting for
it to cool down a bit," said Ben.

Zoe gasped suddenly and adjusted her
goggles to zoom in on the view behind
them. "Something's following us." She
focused on the bare land they'd just
travelled over and frowned. "Can't see
anything now, but I swear there was an
animal on our trail."

Ben grinned as he steered the WASP
round a clump of elephant's trunk plants.
"You're just getting jumpy."

"Hope so," muttered Zoe, keeping watch

over her shoulder. "No, I was right. Something's definitely tracking us."

Ben brought the buggy to a halt and turned. The air shimmered with heat, but in the distance he could see the movement of a large animal. "Can you tell what it is?"

The creature was getting steadily nearer.

"It's all so hazy that's it's hard to see," said Zoe. "Some sort of big cat, I think." She checked the BUG screen. The orange light pulsed in the same place as before. "It's not Jossy's mum because she's still by the well." She refocused her goggles and gulped. "I can see a dark mane. It's a lion and it's big."

Ben gave a low whistle. "It's big all right. But it looks old and scraggy."

"Let's get going and hope he doesn't see us," said Zoe urgently. "Thank goodness for our scent dispersers."

Ben stiffened. "He's raised his snout!" he gasped. "He may not be able to smell *us*,

but I think he's following Jossy's scent."
He hit the accelerator. "Our little friend
here would make a good meal – and we
could be afters!"

Zoe looked anxiously back as their buggy
began to pick up speed. The lion was
bounding towards them and closing the gap
with every second. *Will the WASP be fast
enough to outrun it?* she thought desperately.

They were about to find out.

CHAPTER SIX

Ben changed down a gear, slammed his foot to the floor and the buggy shot forwards.

But the lion was galloping now, sand flying as his pads hit the ground.

"Tranquillize him!" Ben yelled to Zoe. "It's our only hope."

"Can't!" Zoe yelled back, tightening her grip on the cub. "Jossy will fall if I let go."

They hit a small rock, sending a jolt through them all. Jossy gave a mew of pain, which made Zoe feel terrible.

She risked a look back. The cub's cry had

spurred the lion on. "Faster!" she screamed. "He's catching up!"

"We're going as fast as we can," muttered Ben through gritted teeth.

He could see the start of the sand dunes rising up ahead. His heart sank. That would slow them down – he hoped desperately that it would slow the lion even more.

The WASP hit the slope and he rammed his foot down. As it laboured over the sand, he leaned forwards, urging the machine up the hill.

"The lion!" screamed Zoe.

Ben glanced over his shoulder. The creature was in pouncing distance. He could see its sharp teeth as its lip curled in a snarl.

As they reached the top of the hill, the lion leaped, its claws scrabbling at the back of the WASP. At that moment, they surged over the peak and began to accelerate down the steep slope, sand flying all around them.

Zoe twisted in her seat. Panting hard, the lion was trying in vain to keep its footing. Suddenly it looked scrawny and old again.

"You did it," she cried. "We've outrun him!"

"I'm not slowing down yet," Ben yelled back.

They slewed down the dune and up the next, hurtling to the bottom at high speed.

"Watch out!" yelled Zoe.

They were careering towards a stretch of small, sharp boulders. Ben swung the WASP round to avoid them, but it was too late.

KER-RACK! The WASP juddered, lurched to one side and then flipped over.

"Jossy!" yelled Zoe, clambering out of the vehicle and scrambling to her feet. "Is he all right?"

Ben got out and crouched down to examine the motionless cub. "I hope so," he said. "I saw him roll out of your arms, so he didn't fall far."

Zoe ran over, rubbing her grazed elbow. She gently stroked Jossy's head and the cub made a faint mewling sound. "He looks OK, but what about you?" she asked Ben, as she checked the little cub over.

Ben grinned. "Just a few bruises." He went to inspect the WASP. It was lying on its side a little way from them. "Let's see if we can get this back on the road." As he walked round it, Zoe heard him give a low whistle.

"One of the wheels is buckled," he called. "And the axle has snapped. This isn't going anywhere."

"Then we're on foot," said Zoe, hoping she sounded calmer than she felt.

Ben looked back at the way they'd come. "We seem to have lost the lion, thank goodness."

"If we take everything in your backpack," said Zoe, "we can use mine to carry Jossy. No time to hang around here. We'll stop to update Erika once we're absolutely sure the lion's not around any more."

"We need food and water." Ben picked up Zoe's bag and began to empty it. "And the vetkit, of course." He hurriedly unclipped the sail from the WASP. "This will make a good shelter," he told Zoe, as he folded it up and put it in his backpack with their sleeping bags and the rope. "Everything else will have to stay here."

Zoe carefully put Jossy in her backpack. Then she went to help Ben unfasten the water tank. They'd need all the fluid they could carry in this heat.

Suddenly she noticed the dark wet patch on the ground beneath the WASP. She touched it with her fingers and gave a gasp of horror.

"Ben! The tank's damaged. Our water's gone!"

CHAPTER SEVEN

Ben gave the water tank a desperate shake. "There's a little left in the bottom," he said. "Quick, fetch a bottle."

"That's not going to last us long," said Zoe anxiously, as they drained every last drop.

"Then the sooner we get Jossy home the better," declared Ben.

He helped Zoe hoist her backpack on to her shoulders. Zoe felt Jossy's hot little breaths on her neck. "We might go thirsty," she said, "but at least we've got some milk made up for him."

Ben placed the flap of the pack over the cub's head to protect him from the sun. Then he fired a tagging dart into the seat of the WASP and covered the buggy with sand as much as he could. "Erika should be able to find it when our mission's over, but hopefully no one else will."

BUG SAT MAP

OASIS

N

LANDING SITE ✗ ‒ ‒ ‒ ‒ ‒ ‒ ‒ ‒ ‒ ‒

Ben & Zoe's route

Zoe checked the map on her BUG. "Escaping that lion has taken us well off course," she told Ben. "We need to head west now and most of it is over dunes again."

Ben looked at his watch. "It's half past two. We've got about four hours before nightfall. Plenty of time."

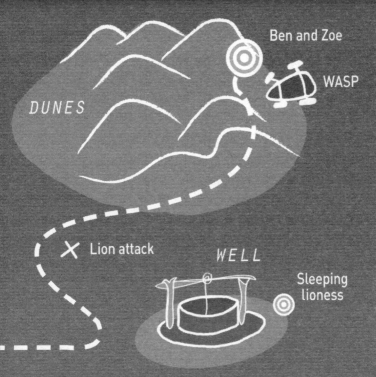

Ben and Zoe

WASP

DUNES

✕ Lion attack

WELL

Sleeping lioness

not to scale

"We won't leave any more trail," said Zoe. "We don't want Jossy's mum catching us up. That last stone was quite a way back so she shouldn't be able to track us. We'll just have to hope she'll head to the pool."

"What's her signal doing?" asked Ben.

"She hasn't moved yet," replied Zoe. "She must still be asleep."

They set off towards the slope of the next dune. The hot sun beat down on them and they could feel the heat of the earth through their boots. A band of ostriches surprised them by belting across their path.

The ridge of the red hill stood out sharp against the blue sky.

"I researched dunes when we were in the plane," Ben told Zoe. "Very interesting – though I didn't think we'd be *walking* over them."

"What's so interesting about piles of sand?" said Zoe, swinging her backpack round to check on the sleeping cub.

"There's more to them than that," replied
Ben. "The steep slope of a dune is called
the slipface and it's really hard to climb.
We're lucky here. We're going up the
gentler side where the sand's firmer."

"Good!" said Zoe, taking the first step on
to the dune. But her leg muscles soon began
to ache as she trudged up the slope.

"And the ripples are where the wind's blown the sand…" Ben went on.

"Thank you, Mr Encyclopedia," groaned his sister. "I'll tell *you* something – the sand's so hot my feet are burning!"

She stopped to shift the straps of the heavy backpack. Jossy snorted in his sleep, right into her ear. A spider scampered across the sand. It stopped and began to dig, burying itself so it could wait for its prey.

I wish we could find cover, thought Zoe.

After a long climb they reached the high ridge. Ahead, long smooth dunes lay in waves across the landscape.

"Amazing!" cried Zoe. "It looks like a huge red ocean." She glanced at the steep slope in front of them. "But how do we get down that?"

"Fancy a race?" asked Ben, with a grin.

"Don't be silly!" said Zoe. "I'd never keep my balance with Jossy on my back."

"You won't have to keep your balance."
Ben sat down, facing the steep slope. "This
isn't called the slipface for nothing. It's
like a slide. We should get up a good
speed, too."

Zoe sat beside him and put
the rucksack on her knees.
"I'm ready."

Ben let out a whoop,
and they pushed off,
sending sand
tumbling after
them as they
went.

"That's the way to go!" said Zoe, shaking sand off her arms at the end of the ride. "Although I didn't expect to travel across the Kalahari on my bottom." She stood up and groaned. "Jossy's feeling really heavy now I'm on my feet again."

"I'll take him for a while," Ben offered.

The children swapped backpacks and made the slow climb up each dune, then slid their way down the slipface on their bottoms. The sun beat down relentlessly and each slope seemed harder than the last.

Zoe flopped on to the sand. "I don't think I can go any further," she puffed. "This heat … it's draining my strength. We need a rest – and water."

With the weight of Jossy dragging on his shoulders, Ben was feeling the strain too, but he wasn't going to worry Zoe. "If we can just make it out of the dunes there might be some shade," he told her, trying to sound cheerful. "We can have a picnic!"

He held out his hand and pulled his sister
to her feet.

Zoe crawled up the slope ahead, licking
her dry lips and trying to drive the image
of cool, fresh water from her mind.

At last she reached Ben at the top.

"No more dunes!" she gasped in relief.

They stared out over the vast stretch of
flat land below, its sparse shrubs and grasses
poking up here and there from the red earth.
With their goggles on full zoom they could
make out a treeline in the far distance, with
an area of vegetation around it.

"That must be the pool," declared Ben.

"But I can't see any shade round here,"
croaked Zoe, her throat feeling like
sandpaper. "Wait! We can shelter under
the sail."

They slid down the last slope and pulled
the sail out. Draping it over their heads,

they made a makeshift tent and flopped down under its welcome shade. Ben eased his pack off and laid it down between them.

Jossy woke up and began to wriggle. Ben offered him some of his milk and he drank thirstily.

Ben grinned at Zoe. "That's a good sign."

"We'd better be careful he doesn't get too lively," said Zoe. "We don't want him escaping."

She took a mouthful of water. She had to force herself not to have any more, but she wanted to drain the bottle dry. She handed it to Ben.

"Better update Erika," said Ben. "She might not be able to land the plane here, but perhaps she could drop us some supplies."

With sweating fingers, Zoe pressed the hot key on her BUG and waited to hear Erika's voice. Nothing happened. "That's strange," muttered Zoe. "It's not connecting.

And now the screen's gone dead."

"Maybe yours is malfunctioning," suggested Ben. He tried his own BUG and shook his head. "Mine's the same – and the tracking and satellite have gone too. I expect it'll come back as we move to a different position. It could be the dunes affecting it."

But Zoe wasn't listening. She was staring in delight at the ground a few metres in front of them.

Ben looked up to see a group of small, skinny brown creatures with big dark eyes, scurrying around. "Meerkats!" he whispered.

They watched the busy group sniffing and digging, tossing up the earth behind them. The babies tumbled about, biting each other playfully. Two large adults stood bolt upright on a nearby rock. Their heads swivelled this way and that, checking the area for signs of danger.

Ben looked at his sister and grinned. "Off
in the land of gooeyness," he groaned.

"But they're so sweet!" sighed Zoe. "Look
at that little one playing with his friend's
tail."

Jossy gave a loud mew and tried to get out
of the backpack. Ben laughed. "You can't go
and play with them!"

Suddenly, one of the lookouts gave a shrill cry and in a second every meerkat had vanished into burrows in the ground.

"They're frightened," said Zoe, glancing around. "Were they scared of Jossy, do you think?"

Ben shaded his eyes and looked up. "Might have been an eagle. Sorry your little friends have scampered off, but at least we can get going again." He swung his backpack up on to his shoulders and Jossy pushed a paw out and batted at the flap of his hat.

Zoe was pointing straight ahead. "That's why the meerkats ran off," she cried.

Ben followed her gaze. A swirling orange wall was eating up the land, moving slowly closer and closer. "Sandstorm," he gasped. "And we're right in its path."

"Remember our training in the Wild climate chamber," said Zoe urgently, pulling out two cotton scarves. When they'd both covered their noses and mouths she tightened her grasp on the WASP sail. "We must face away from the storm," she urged Ben. The sail flapped madly in the hot, dry wind that was becoming stronger every moment. As they pulled the makeshift shelter right over them they felt the sand beating at the metallic fabric.

Ben crouched down to join her. Wide awake now, Jossy wriggled out of the backpack. Ben grabbed at him with one hand, but the little cub squirmed free. In the next instant he had disappeared into the storm.

CHAPTER EIGHT

With a cry of alarm, Zoe dived out into the swirling storm. She felt the sand beating on her, stinging her hands like sharp needles. Bent double, she stumbled around, calling for Jossy. But her voice was muffled by the cotton covering her mouth and lost in the howling wind.

He's not a trained animal, she thought to herself in desperation. *He won't come to my call, but he must be somewhere near. He might even have gone back to the shelter.* She turned, but couldn't see the sail any longer.

She was totally lost.

Zoe fought down her rising panic as she crept on, trying to find something to focus on – anything that would tell her where she was. But she couldn't make out any landmarks, only swirling sand. She should have stayed in the shelter with Ben. But she knew she'd had no choice. She had to find Jossy.

The sand was driving at her face now, coming straight at her goggles. She began to feel dizzy as she watched its swirling movement. She took an uncertain step forward, stumbled and fell heavily. As she stretched out her hand to pick herself up she felt her fingers come into contact with something alive.

Zoe's instincts kicked in. She withdrew her hand quickly and curled up, arms over her head, fearing an attack. She could hear something crying out – or growling, she

wasn't sure which in the deafening storm.
But suddenly there was a nose nudging at
her arm. Zoe risked a peek. A familiar face
was staring down into hers.

"Jossy!" she exclaimed, clasping the
trembling cub tightly and curling round
him as the sand swept over them. "I've got
you. You're all right now."

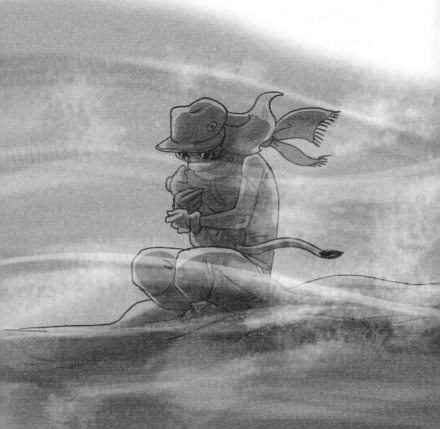

The lion cub seemed to sense that he had reached safety. He lay in Zoe's arms, sneezing and shaking his head to free himself of the fine sand.

If only she could contact Ben on her BUG and tell him she'd found Jossy, but all Zoe could do now was to wait until the storm moved on. And she had no idea how long that would be.

Ben lay under his shelter, fighting down the urge to go to Zoe's rescue. He admired her courage in going after Jossy, but she'd taken their mission too far. The sound of the sand beating on his shelter was deafening, and, as the wind whipped round, it caught the corners of the sail so that he struggled to hold it. He could feel the sand beginning to cover him, first his feet, then his back. He kept shaking it off – horrified at the thought of being buried alive.

After what felt like an eternity, the sound of the storm began to die away. Ben cautiously raised a corner of the sail and looked out. Zoe was nowhere to be seen, and nor was Jossy. The air grew still and ahead of him lay the blown sand, banked up in smooth slopes and mounds against trees, and round bushes and rocks.

A terrible thought came to him. Was Zoe somewhere under there, struggling for breath?

Ben jumped as he heard a shout close behind him. He leaped to his feet, threw the sail aside and swung round. Just a few paces away lay a shallow bank of sand. Zoe was emerging from the far side – with Jossy in her arms!

Ben gave a whoop of relief, ripped off his goggles and cotton scarf and ran towards his sister.

"That was scary!" called Zoe, uncovering her face. "If only I'd known I was so close. But I found our naughty little friend!"

"Not sure who was the naughty one," said Ben sternly. "You should never have left the shelter in those conditions."

"I know," admitted Zoe. "But if I hadn't, we might have lost Jossy for good."

Ben grinned. "And you say I'm the one who takes the risks!"

Jossy wriggled in Zoe's arms. "OK, boy," she said soothingly. "We're going now."

Ben reached out and stroked the cub to help calm him. Then he looked up at the sky. Over in the west the sun was beginning to sink towards the dunes. "We won't get much further before nightfall," he said. "We ought to set up camp and make for the pool in the morning."

"Good idea." Zoe wiped her mouth with her hand. "And I need some water! I'm really dry after that storm – and I bet Jossy could do with a drink too."

Ben held up the water bottle and shook it. "Not much here," he said. He saw the look of alarm on Zoe's face. "Don't worry – we'll think of something. There are a few plants growing here so there must be water somewhere."

"I've just remembered something I saw on TV," said Zoe. "A programme about the bushmen of the Kalahari. They dug up melons and drank the fluid inside. They had leaves a bit like dandelions and the melons were on long stalks under the surface."

"Let's get digging," exclaimed Ben.

Jossy seemed sleepy again now so they made him comfortable in the backpack and began their search. There were clumps of yellow spiky grass and thorn bushes pushing up through the newly laid sand, but no sign of the dandelion-like leaves.

The sun was very low now, and sinking fast. Zoe began to scrape away the sand, trying to ignore the overwhelming dryness in her mouth.

They searched and dug until darkness fell, but they didn't find anything.

"Time to stop," said Ben, running his tongue over his dry lips. It didn't help. "We're not getting anywhere. I reckon the sandstorm's hidden any melon leaves. We should get some sleep."

"Agreed," said Zoe wearily. "I'm even thirstier now."

Ben handed her their water bottle. "There's about three sips each so make the most of it!"

Zoe felt the drops of warm water disappear in her dry mouth. She took out Jossy's milk. The little lion cub looked at her drowsily as she gently pushed the teat between his teeth. He began to suck. Before Zoe knew what had happened the bottle was empty.

"He's had it all!" she said in alarm. "There's none left. What are we going to do?"

"Don't worry," Ben told her. "There'll be more by morning. I've just had an idea."

He pulled the sail across the sand and draped it over a couple of nearby bushes, letting it dip in the middle. "We'll sleep under here, and we'll find water in that hollow when we wake up."

"I'm not falling for that one, Ben," said Zoe. "It's not likely to rain in the night."

"But there will be condensation," explained Ben. "The moisture in the air will condense on the sail and run down into the hollow."

Ben heaved the backpacks under the shelter, crawled in and pulled out an energy bar. "At least we've got a bit of food left."

It was hard to eat the energy bar without a drink. It stuck to the roofs of their mouths. Zoe could feel her lips cracking and gave up. She wrapped the bar up, half eaten and put it away. Ben wasn't doing much better.

He took up his BUG. "It's working now the storm's passed," he said, tapping at the buttons. "I've told Erika we'll be at the pool in the morning ... and she says contact her again then."

Zoe looked down at the little lion cub. His head was on his paws and his eyes were closed. "I'll check on your mother," she told him, "and see how far she's got."

But when the signal appeared on her screen, Zoe's face fell. "She still hasn't moved, Ben." She gulped hard.

"I think I've killed her."

CHAPTER NINE

"I'm sure the lioness is fine," said Ben, putting his arm round his sister. "She probably woke up just after we left and has made her way back to the pride."

"Then why is her signal still in the same place?" Zoe gulped, as she tried to hold back the tears. "I've given her too much tranquillizer. I should've known. She'll be at risk from predators – maybe even that male lion."

Ben gave her a friendly nudge. "It's probably your BUG getting it wrong.

It might still be playing up."

Zoe managed a wobbly smile. "That could be it," she said. "I'm being silly..."

She broke off as a strange wailing sound filled the air all around them. "What's that?" she gasped, clutching Ben's arm. She peered out over the sand. It was dark now and she felt herself shiver. "It's so creepy. Like spooky musical instruments."

"Ghosts of the Kalahari!" said Ben, his eyes wide.

"Don't be silly," whispered Zoe. "It can't be ... can it?"

"Phantoms of travellers lost in the desert," Ben went on in a sinister voice. "Searching for victims."

Zoe gave a shriek.

"Or is it just a bunch of camels playing clarinets?" Ben went on.

Zoe looked at him. "You know what it really is, don't you?"

Ben grinned at her. "It's the sand singing! I read about it on the plane. It happens here in the desert when the wind has dropped."

Zoe punched her brother's arm. "How can the sand make that noise?" she asked.

"The wind drives the sand up the dunes," Ben explained. "But in the end the top gets too heavy and starts to slide. That's what we can hear."

"Weird!" said Zoe. "You wouldn't expect it to be so eerie." She shivered and moved closer to her brother, as the dull song echoed round. "Temperature's dropping." She looked out from under the shelter up at the black sky. It was filled with bright stars. "No cloud cover," she murmured. "It's going to be a cold night."

Ben checked the little cub's leg wound by torchlight. "Looks clean," he reported. "Let's get some sleep."

He unfolded their sleeping bags and they curled up as close to each other as they could.

"Jossy makes a nice hot-water bottle," said Zoe, as the little cub settled down beside her.

In the distance she could hear cries as nocturnal creatures called to each other. She checked that the scent disperser was still working on her BUG and then analyzed the calls.

"Jackals," she told Ben. "Leopard, genets, hyenas! It's predator city out there."

"This could be a problem," said Ben. "They won't smell us but they might catch Jossy's scent. We need a deterrent."

"One of us stays awake with the tranquillizer gun?" suggested Zoe.

"No need!" said Ben. He tapped some keys on his BUG and aimed a hologram image of a crackling fire just beyond their shelter. "That should keep them away."

Jossy suddenly wriggled and scratched his ear. He looked around, interested by the distant calls.

"Better make sure he doesn't wander off again," said Zoe. She took the rope from Ben's backpack and fastened it round Jossy's body in a harness, tying the other end firmly to her wrist. "Now if you make a break for it, you'll be dragging me with you!"

She stroked the cub's back and he rubbed his cheek against her face. "He's such a darling," she cooed. "I wish I could keep him." She caught sight of her brother rolling his eyes in mock despair. "I know I can't," she said with a grin.

Jossy snuggled down and was soon breathing deeply, his paws twitching as he dreamed.

Zoe huddled closer to the warm cub. The air on her face was getting very cold and she began to wish that the hologram image of the fire was real. She pulled her sleeping bag around her ears. Ben was already asleep, but Zoe couldn't settle. The creepy song of the sands was still echoing in the distance – zombies or ghouls coming from the grave. *Don't be silly!* she told herself. *Think of something else.* But that brought her back to fretting about the lioness again. She was sure that the amount of tranquillizer had been correct, but why hadn't the signal moved? As her anxious thoughts whirled around her head, Zoe felt like she'd never sleep…

The next thing she knew, Zoe found herself at the top of a sand dune ready to toboggan down towards a huge pool of cool, inviting water. She jumped on her sledge and was about to launch herself off when Gran appeared, grabbed her wrist and tugged it hard.

Zoe jerked awake. The sky outside their shelter was shot with orange and purple as if it was on fire. She peered at it, puzzled.

It's dawn! she realized. She'd been dreaming. Of course Gran wasn't here with them. There was no pool and she was thirstier than she'd ever felt in her life.

But something was pulling at her wrist. She hadn't been dreaming that.

She sat up and looked about her. It was Jossy tugging at his lead! The little cub was scampering about at her feet, limping slightly on his bad leg. He nosed the ground, pawed at a small, dark object and jumped back.

"You're better," said Zoe. "That looks like playing to me."

She gave Ben a nudge. He stirred and gazed blankly at her, his hair sticking up.

"Whasss-going-on?" he muttered, rubbing his eyes.

"Our patient's making a good recovery," Zoe told him. "He's playing a game."

Ben focused on the cub. "What's he got there?" he asked.

Jossy pounced again and lifted his paw, ready to cuff the thing on the sand.

With a moment of cold dread, Zoe saw what it was.

"It's a scorpion!" she cried. "And its tail's up. It's about to strike!"

CHAPTER TEN

Zoe yanked at Jossy's rope, dragging him towards her. But the angry scorpion darted after him.

Ben was out of his sleeping bag like a shot. He crouched down, fumbling with one hand for his hat. *I'll trap it*, he thought.

But where was his hat? He didn't dare take his eyes off the scorpion. It had stopped, tail twitching, in easy reach of Jossy. At last, Ben's fingers closed on the brim of his cap. He snatched it up and slammed it over the scorpion.

Zip! The sting appeared through the material.

"Wow!" Ben gave a gasp, as he whipped his hand away just in time. "That was close!"

He flipped the cap over, catching the scorpion inside. Then he swung it like a racket and sent the poisonous insect flying far from their camp.

"We could have done with some meerkats," he went on. "They're immune to the stings and they'd have had it for breakfast."

"They're welcome to it," said Zoe, with a shudder. She was finding it hard to speak because her mouth was so dry.

Ben was panting from his exertions. *I shouldn't be feeling like this*, he thought. *I'm getting dehydrated.*

The sun was now peeking over the distant dunes. Ben crawled out to inspect the roof of their shelter.

"Look at this," he gasped. "It worked!"

The two children each scooped up a handful of the cold water that lay in the dip of the sail and gulped it down.

"No more!" warned Ben. "We have to save the rest for later."

Ben held the sail carefully, while Zoe collected every drop of the precious fluid in their bottles. They used some to make Jossy a little of his special milk, then stowed the bottles in Ben's backpack.

"Better get moving," said Ben. "It's going to be hot soon."

He turned off the fire hologram and pulled his backpack towards him. A trailing strap attracted Jossy's attention and he pounced on it with a small growl. Grasping it in his front paws, he rolled over on to his back and bit at it. Then he jumped to his feet and scampered round in circles.

"That's a good sign," said Zoe. "He doesn't seem to be in any pain from that wound and it looks like it's healing well."

Ben grinned at the little cub's antics. It hurt his cracked lips, but he was pleased to see that Jossy was feeling better. "We'll have to keep him on his lead or he'll be off all over the place. He's certainly not going to let us put him in a backpack."

Zoe grabbed the rope. "Here, Jossy!" she called. She dangled the end in front of him and he swiped at it.

"I might have to play like this all the way," she told Ben.

Ben called up the map on his BUG. "It's west to the pool and it shouldn't take more than an hour."

"What about his mum's signal?" asked Zoe, anxiously. She'd forgotten about her for the moment, with the scare of the scorpion. She brought up the tracking screen. "Oh no," she groaned. "She's still at the well." Zoe tested the BUG's other functions just to be sure. "This is working fine so she must still be there."

Ben squeezed her arm. "We'll get Erika to take us back there after we've delivered Jossy," he told her. He flicked through the menu. "Now I'm setting my BUG to pick up lion cries. Then we'll know that we're taking our little charge to the right place."

Zoe pulled firmly on the lead. "Come on, Jossy. Let's get you home."

They packed up and set off across the flat, hard-baked earth, allowing themselves occasional sips of water from their small supply. The dunes were behind them now. Shading his eyes, Ben could make out a herd of wildebeest far away, bunching round a small patch of green. The sky was a deep turquoise with tiny white clouds. And it was very hot. He felt his head swimming, but he knew he had to keep going.

Jossy scampered along, pulling at the lead and sniffing at every plant and rock.

"Not long now, Jossy," said Zoe. "Has the BUG picked up any lion cries?" she asked her brother.

Ben shook his head. "Nothing on the screen yet. But that doesn't mean they're not near. They could be asleep."

They reached the bottom of a stony ridge. At that moment they heard a scraping noise and a shower of pebbles came rolling down towards them. They looked up to see a large antelope standing proudly at the top.

"Awesome," whispered Zoe.

"It's a gemsbok," Ben whispered back. "Did you know it can raise its body temperature above normal so it doesn't waste energy panting?"

Zoe smothered a giggle. "I can always rely on you for an important fact."

Jossy had seen the gemsbok now. He gave an excited mew and tried to scramble towards the ridge.

With a scuffle of hooves, the creature had gone.

"I think our little cub's hungry," said Ben. "He wants to do a bit of hunting. He really is feeling better. Let's get to the top of this ridge and check out the view. We might spot the pride."

"We have to be careful," replied Zoe. "We don't want them spotting us first."

They crept up to the top of the ridge and scanned the terrain ahead. The gemsbok was bounding down towards his herd, which was grazing under a baobab tree. Beyond the tree a group of buffalo wandered across the grassy sand.

"There's the pool!" said Ben, pointing at a circle of trees in the distance, bright green against the orange land. "Over to the west."

Zoe bent down and scratched Jossy between the ears. "Nearly home," she said. "At least I hope so. I can't see any lions."

Ben checked his BUG. "It's picking up lion cries now," he said. "And they're definitely coming from those trees. I reckon we've found Jossy's family."

They set off down the ridge. Something was lying on the ground ahead.

"It's a dead gemsbok," said Ben as they got near. "Predators have been here. What's the betting it's the lions? Not nice to see, but everything has to eat."

Jossy sniffed the air eagerly and pulled hard at the rope.

"He's hungry," said Zoe. "Is he old enough to eat meat?"

"He seems keen enough," answered Ben. "Let's give it a try."

Whatever had killed the gemsbok had fed well, but there was still some meat left. Jossy pulled Zoe over and began to eat hungrily.

"He's going to be OK," said Zoe. "I can't believe our mission's nearly complete."

A low chuckling sound behind her made her spin round.

"Ben!" she said quickly. "We're in trouble."

He turned and froze. A band of bristling hyenas was slinking menacingly towards them.

CHAPTER ELEVEN

The hyenas held their heads and ears high
and the ridges of spotted hair on their backs
were stiff with aggression. The leader made
a growling whoop in its throat and they
began to circle the children.

"I think this was going to be their
breakfast," whispered Zoe.

"And now we could be!" Ben whispered
back.

Jossy stopped eating and edged away from
the snarling pack.

Ben slowly lifted his tranquillizer gun

and set the dose. Then he lowered his arm.
"There's no way I can shoot them all," he
muttered out of the corner of his mouth.
"We need to try something else. We have to
be more aggressive than them." He waved
his arms wildly and stamped towards the
pack, making loud growling noises.

Zoe joined in. The hyenas stopped their
advance and eyed the children warily.

"It's not enough," said Ben urgently. "I'm
going to try something else."

He took his BUG and was searching for
the setting to make it roar like a lion when
a deep-throated sound boomed out all
around them.

The leader of the pack gave a high-
pitched yowl and the hyenas immediately
scattered, bounding away across the desert.

Ben looked at Zoe in amazement. "Was
that your BUG?" he said. "It certainly did
the trick. Well done."

Zoe was gazing, transfixed, over his shoulder. He saw her eyes flicker with fear.

"It wasn't me," she whispered. She pointed up at the ridge. Ben turned slowly round.

A huge lion with a magnificent black mane was standing at the top of the ridge. It lifted its head and gave another tremendous roar.

Ben and Zoe dived for cover behind a rock, dragging Jossy with them. The lion stalked slowly towards their hiding place, growling deeply.

Jossy began to mew loudly.

"Shhh!" hissed Zoe in desperation. "You'll give us away!" With a trembling hand she slowly stroked Jossy's head, trying to calm him. But the little cub mewed all the louder, wriggling to break free.

The lion stopped in his tracks, ears twitching as he tried to track the sound. Then his gaze fell on the rock. Slowly and purposefully he padded towards it.

Suddenly, Jossy wriggled out of his harness and broke away from Zoe's hold. The cub bounded towards the lion, giving little growls as he went.

Ben fumbled desperately with his gun, his fingers slipping on the trigger. "I think he's trying to protect us," he said in horror.

"Come back!" called Zoe. "You're too small, Jossy. You don't stand a chance."

But Jossy scampered between the lion's legs and began playfully biting his tail!

Then he rolled over on his back and batted it. The huge creature looked down at him.

Ben edged round the rock. He got a firm grip on the gun, raised it and took aim.

Zoe caught his arm. "Wait," she cried. "I think Jossy's going to be all right."

Instead of attacking the little cub, the huge lion gave him a friendly cuff with his paw.

Ben lowered the gun and grinned. "There's only one male lion who would accept that behaviour from Jossy," he said. "It must be his dad! And from the deep colour of his mane I'd say he's the dominant male."

"Then it must be Jossy's pride at the pool," said Zoe eagerly. "I hope the mum's there." She looked at the tracking screen on her BUG. The orange light was still static at the well. "She's still not moved," Zoe whispered. "I'm really worried about her, Ben."

"I bet she's fine," said Ben, trying to sound confident. But he could see that Zoe didn't look convinced. "Look!" he went on. "Jossy and his dad are on the move."

The male lion had turned and was striding away towards the distant trees around the pool. Jossy trotted along at his side, nipping at his leg until his father butted him off. The little cub went rolling across the red earth, jumped to his feet and scampered alongside his dad.

"Let's follow," said Ben. "We have to report that he's safely back with the pride."

"Who's going to look after him if his mum isn't there?" asked Zoe.

"I don't think that'll be a problem," said
Ben. "All the females help each other to
rear their cubs. They're like aunties."

Keeping their distance, they followed the
lions towards the pool. When they reached
the trees, they moved cautiously forwards,
keeping out of sight behind the branches.

"Wow!" whispered Zoe.

The pool was as big as a football pitch.
It was completely surrounded by palm trees,

baobabs and camel's thorns with their ferny leaves. Water glinted in the harsh sunlight as it rippled at the banks. Grass and small flowers grew under the trees and the air was full of bird cries and song.

Ben pointed over to the far side. Stretched out on a sandbank was a group of lions. Some were asleep and others were crouched at the water, drinking. Several young cubs were playing together in the shade.

"I've counted fifteen," whispered Ben. "That's not a bad size for a pride of lions under threat."

Jossy and his dad walked over to the group and at once a lioness sprang up.

"Is that his mum?" whispered Zoe.

"If it is he'll go straight to her," said Ben.

Now other lionesses were on their feet, all nosing round the baby. But Jossy trotted from one to the other as if searching.

"She's not there," said Zoe, close to tears. "And it's all my fault."

CHAPTER TWELVE

Jossy finally flopped down next to a scrawny old lioness. She sniffed him suspiciously all over.

"Do you think he smells strange to her?" asked Zoe. "He's been away from the pride for a while. I hope he doesn't get rejected."

"No chance," said Ben. The female was now giving Jossy a thorough licking. He leaned against her as she flattened his ears and pushed him this way and that. Wash over, Jossy jumped up and began to search again amongst the females.

"We've got him home, but not his mum," said Zoe. She felt incredibly sad.

Ben put his arm round her. "It's not your fault," he said kindly. "And anyway, the other females are making sure Jossy's going to be OK. He'll be fine." He took his BUG, put it on loudspeaker and hit the hot key for Erika.

"Hello there," came her voice. "How's the mission going?"

"The cub's back with the pride—" Ben reported.

"But we don't know where his mother is," Zoe burst out. "I had to tranquillize her and..."

She gulped and Ben told Erika all that had happened.

"Your godfather will be proud of you," said Erika. "And Zoe, try not to worry. You did all you could for the lioness."

"The moment you pick us up, can we go

to the well to see what's happened to her?" asked Zoe.

"Of course," said Erika. "I'll land as close to you as I can. It won't take you long on the WASP to get to the plane. I'll send you the co-ordinates. And I've got plenty of water so you'll soon be feeling better."

"Ah … yes…" said Ben hesitantly. "About the WASP, Erika. I'm afraid we had a little mishap." He told her about the encounter with the hungry lion.

"Then I'll arrange some other transport," said Erika. "See you soon!"

They sat in the shelter of the trees and watched as Jossy finally settled down next to the female who had washed him and began to suckle. But he kept stopping to look around for his mum. The other cubs began a tumbling game while the adults stretched out sleepily as the heat of the day increased.

Ben and Zoe sipped at their remaining
water and ate an energy bar. It was getting
very hot. Zoe felt her eyelids droop.

Suddenly her BUG vibrated.

"I'm here – due south of you," came
Erika's voice. "I've made sure I'm safely
upwind of the lions."

"Why would she worry about the lions
picking up her scent?" asked Ben. "She's got
a scent disperser, hasn't she?"

Zoe shaded her eyes and peered ahead.
"It's not herself she's worried about," she
told Ben, pointing. "It's our transport!"

Ben followed her gaze and gave a groan.
"I might have known it would be camels!"

"We're on our way," Zoe told Erika. "Over
and out." Zoe didn't say anything to Ben,
but inside she felt empty. She couldn't
escape the horrible thought that she had
killed Jossy's mum.

At that moment, a high-pitched mewling

had them looking back towards the pride.

Jossy had left the group, crying excitedly
as he ran towards something approaching in
the distance.

The other lions were up and staring.

"It's a lioness," whispered Ben.

The newcomer was limping slowly
towards the water. She had scratches on her
side and her muzzle was bleeding. She
stopped when she saw Jossy and made a
deep rumbling noise.

Jossy threw himself at her, running between her legs and buffeting her sides. The lioness slumped to the ground and Jossy crept between her front paws, nudging her face with his.

"It's his mum," exclaimed Zoe in delight.

"She looks like she's been fighting," said Ben. "I wonder if she came upon that lone male like we did. It would explain why she's taken so long to get here."

They drank in the scene of the reunion. Jossy climbed happily all over his weary mother, kneading at her like a kitten with his claws. She nuzzled him and rubbed her cheeks against his. The other lionesses padded round them, sniffing and licking at her wounds.

"I can't believe she's made it back!" said Zoe, her eyes shining, as at last the pride settled down and the little cub curled up contentedly next to his mum.

Zoe turned to Ben. "But why didn't her
dart show on the BUG?"

Ben checked the BUG screen and showed
his sister. "It *is* showing," Ben insisted with
a grin. "You must have missed and tracked
the well!" He jumped to his feet and tugged
at Zoe's arm. "Time to go. Erika's waiting."

"Do we have to?" sighed Zoe. "I could

watch the lions for ever."

"And miss the chance of seeing me fall off another camel?" joked Ben.

Zoe got to her feet and took one last look back. "Bye, Jossy," she whispered. "I'm so glad you're safely home." Then the children crept away quietly through the trees.

As they approached Erika, Ben's BUG vibrated. "It's a call from Wild," he said.

"Greetings!" came their godfather's cheerful voice. "Erika's brought me up to speed. Well done!"

"You're not quite up to speed," called Zoe, happily. "Jossy's mum's back! She made it after all."

"Then it's a perfect end to a perfect mission!" declared Uncle Stephen.

Ben gazed ahead to where one of the camels was snorting and stamping its hoof. "Almost perfect!" He laughed.

AFRICAN LION SURVIVAL

Lions are found mainly in the sub Saharan region of Africa. They live in savannahs, grasslands, dense bush and woodlands.

No. of lions living in the wild in Africa ⟶ about 21,000

Life span: 10-14 years in wild • Over 20 years in captivity – have been known to live to 25 years

Length from head to tail – Males 170–250 cm • Females 140–175 cm
Weight – 150–227kg (males)

Females are pregnant for 110 days and have between 1-4 cubs.

They give birth in a secluded den, such as a cave. They keep to themselves while the cubs are helpless. They move dens several times during this time to keep the scent from building up and attracting other predators. They usually return to the pride when the cubs are about six weeks old.

At birth, the cubs weigh between 1.2 –2.1kg.

Weaning happens at 6–7 months.

STATUS: VULNERABLE

Over the last 30 years Africa has lost 70% of its lions.

RESCUE

THREATS

PREDATORS

Lions have no natural predators. Man is the biggest threat to their survival. Outside the national parks there are more and more encounters between lion and human, as the human population increases.

POISONING

Livestock owners whose animals are killed by lions sprinkle animal carcasses with a strong poison as a bait to the lions. They will also shoot them.

HUNTING

The lion is one of the 'big five' prized by hunters.

HABITAT LOSS

People are taking over lion territory, which causes conflict between humans and lions.

Although known as the King of the Jungle, lions prefer open savannah country. The Namibian lion lives in a harsh habitat of gravel plains and basalt mountains. They can survive without drinking water and they feed on gemsboks, ostriches, and occasionally even seals. Females do almost all the hunting, usually working together.

It's not all bad news!

Many lions live in protected national parks. Conservation groups are working hard to preserve the numbers of lions. For instance, the African Wildlife Foundation has lion conservation research projects in Tanzania and Botswana.

J. BURCHETT & S. VOGLER

WILD
RESCUE
EARTHQUAKE ESCAPE

Following a massive earthquake, an orphaned giant panda has escaped from a sanctuary in China's Sichuan Province. Not only is he at risk of attack from leopards, but it seems he may have strayed into an area where all the bamboo has died. With the panda cub now in danger of starvation, it's up to Ben and Zoe to rescue him.

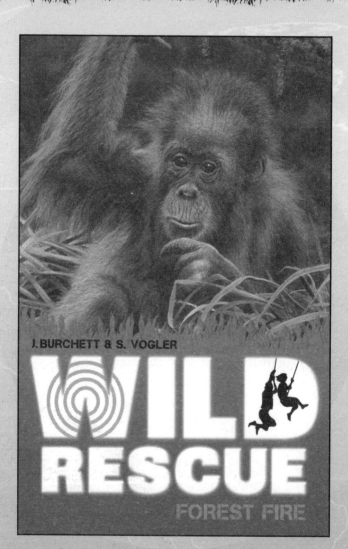

J. BURCHETT & S. VOGLER

WILD RESCUE

FOREST FIRE

Ben and Zoe's latest mission takes them to South Borneo. An orang-utan has set up home on a palm oil plantation and is resisting all attempts to bring him to the safety of the nearby reservation. But when they discover that illegal logging has been taking place, it becomes clear that the orang-utan isn't the only one in grave danger.

J. BURCHETT & S. VOGLER

WILD
RESCUE
POLAR MELTDOWN

Following reports of a polar bear shot dead near an Alaskan village, Uncle Stephen is sending Ben and Zoe to the scene. It seems that the dead bear had recently given birth. This means there are orphaned cubs out there. If Ben and Zoe don't get to them soon, the cubs won't stand a chance. But the young polar bears could be anywhere and there is a vicious storm brewing...

J. BURCHETT & S. VOGLER

WILD RESCUE

SAFARI SURVIVAL

Ben and Zoe are off to a game reserve in the Kenyan savannah, where some tourists are paying big money to illegally hunt elephants for "sport". The latest visitor has his sights set on a mother and baby elephant… The race is on for Ben and Zoe to track down the vulnerable elephants before the hunters do. Will they get there in time?

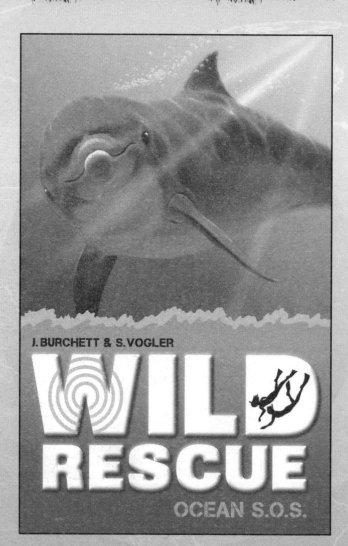

J. BURCHETT & S. VOGLER

WILD RESCUE

OCEAN S.O.S.

For their latest mission, Ben and Zoe are on their way to the Caribbean, following reports that an unscrupulous marine park has dumped a young dolphin into the ocean. Because the dolphin was born in captivity, he is unprepared for life in the open sea. Now Ben and Zoe must guide the defenceless dolphin to safety, before he finds himself in dangerous waters...

J. BURCHETT & S. VOGLER

WILD RESCUE

AVALANCHE ALERT

Ben and Zoe's skills are put to the test when they are dispatched to the treacherous slopes of the Himalayas. Following an avalanche, a mother snow leopard and one of her cubs have been cut off from their territory, leaving her two other cubs to fend for themselves. It's down to the children to brave sub-zero temperatures and sheer rock faces, and lead the mother and her cub home.

If you want to find out more
about lions, visit:

www.wwf.org.uk
www.awf.org
www.desertlion.info

Moon Bear

Gill Lewis

OXFORD
UNIVERSITY PRESS

OXFORD
UNIVERSITY PRESS

Great Clarendon Street, Oxford OX2 6DP
Oxford University Press is a department of the University of Oxford.
It furthers the University's objective of excellence in research, scholarship,
and education by publishing worldwide in

Oxford   New York

Auckland   Cape Town   Dar es Salaam   Hong Kong   Karachi
Kuala Lumpur   Madrid   Melbourne   Mexico City   Nairobi
New Delhi   Shanghai   Taipei   Toronto

With offices in

Argentina   Austria   Brazil   Chile   Czech Republic   France   Greece
Guatemala   Hungary   Italy   Japan   Poland   Portugal   Singapore
South Korea   Switzerland   Thailand   Turkey   Ukraine   Vietnam

Oxford is a registered trade mark of Oxford University Press
in the UK and in certain other countries

British Library Cataloguing in Publication Data
Data available

ISBN: 978-0-19-279354-6
1 3 5 7 9 10 8 6 4 2

Printed in Great Britain

Paper used in the production of this book is a natural,
recyclable product made from wood grown in sustainable forests.
The manufacturing process conforms to the environmental
regulations of the country of origin.